For Tazzi and Harriet, with thanks
A.M.

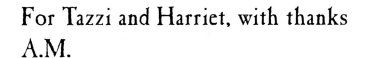

Dedication
E.T.

LINCOLNSHIRE COUNTY COUNCIL	
04016452	
PETERS	£10.99
26-Jul-05	JPIC

First published in Great Britain in 2005 by
Gullane Children's Books,
an imprint of Pinwheel Limited
Winchester House, 259-269 Old Marylebone Road,
London NW1 5XJ

1 3 5 7 9 10 8 6 4 2

Text © Angela McAllister 2005
Illustrations © Eleanor Taylor 2005

ISBN 1-86233-556-7

Printed and bound in China

Big Yang
and Little Yin

Angela McAllister Eleanor Taylor

GULLANE
CHILDREN'S BOOKS

Big Yang and Little Yin were playing brave explorers.

"Let's explore the forest," said Little Yin.
"Yes, that's the place for adventures!" said Big Yang.
So Little Yin put her snugly into her trolley,
and off they went.

Soon they found a perfect
tree to climb.
Big Yang pulled Little Yin up
onto the lowest branch.
"I want to climb higher," said
brave Little Yin.

And with Big Yang's help she did.

Then they found a stream.
"Let's make a raft," said Big Yang. So they
turned the trolley upside down. Big brave Yang
paddled the raft round the rocks.

After a while they stopped to pick some berries.
All around, the forest creaked and rustled.
"What's that?" whispered Little Yin.

"Don't worry," said Big Yang.
"There aren't any fierce animals in this forest."
"Oh, brave explorers aren't afraid of
fierce animals," said Little Yin.

Deeper into the woods they went.
Big Yang made them a den.
Dark shadows shifted between the trees.
"Who's there?" whispered Little Yin.

"Don't worry," said Big Yang. "There
aren't any witches in this wood."
"Oh, brave explorers aren't afraid of
witches," said Little Yin.

Further on, they came to an enormous hollow tree.
Little Yin climbed up and peered into the trunk.
"I think it's a monster's house,"
she said in her explorer's voice.
But suddenly she wobbled and
dropped her snugly inside.

"Don't worry," said
Big Yang. "I'll get it for you!"

Big Yang climbed into the
hollow tree and found the snugly.
But he couldn't climb out.

"Help!" cried Big Yang.

Little Yin peeped through a hole.
"Don't worry," she said.
"I'll get some help."

Little Yin looked around
the deep, dark forest.
"Are you afraid?" asked Big Yang.
"Um . . . brave explorers are never
afraid," said Little Yin, with a shiver.

Big Yang grabbed his mittens and
threw them out of the tree. "Take these,
Little Yin," he said. "They'll keep you warm."

Little Yin set off
through the forest.
She came to
Big Yang's den.
Spooky shadows
danced all around.

Suddenly Little Yin
didn't feel brave any
more. She tried
to sing a loud,
witch-frightening
song, but her voice
was very small.

In the hollow tree
Big Yang sat alone,
peeping through
the hole. "Maybe this
is a monster's house,"
he said to himself
"and maybe he comes
home for lunch..."

Suddenly Big Yang
didn't feel so brave.
He tried to hum a
loud, monster-scaring
hum, but his voice
was very wobbly.

Little Yin stumbled on until she found the berry bush.
The wind howled through the forest like a fierce animal.
"I don't want to be an explorer any more," said Little Yin.
"I'm only brave with Big Yang to look after me."

But Big Yang was huddled in the hollow tree.
What if Little Yin forgets where to find me! he thought.
Big Yang didn't want to be an explorer any more. "I'm
only brave with Little Yin to look after," he said.

Little Yin sat trembling
in a burrow of leaves.
Then she remembered
Big Yang's mittens.
She put them on.

The mittens were
warm and cosy.
Little Yin smiled. She
felt as though Big Yang
was holding her hand.
Up she got. "I can do
it," she said bravely.
"I must find help.
Don't worry, Big Yang."
And on she went.

Inside the tree, a teardrop rolled down Big Yang's cheek. He picked up the snugly to wipe his eye.

It was soft and cuddly and it smelt of Little Yin.
Big Yang smiled. He felt as if Little Yin was beside him.
"I'm not really worried," said Big Yang bravely.
"Little Yin will be here soon." And he practised his alphabet to cheer himself up.

Before long Little Yin came to the stream and there was her trolley, still upside down. She had forgotten all about it. "This is just what we need!" cried Little Yin happily.

When Big Yang heard the rattling wheels he jumped up.
"Little Yin!" he cried.
"The trolley! How clever!"
"Will it help?" asked Little Yin.
"It's *perfect*!" said Big Yang.

Big Yang threw the end
of the snugly to Little
Yin and she tied it on
to the trolley.

Together they pushed and
pulled the trolley inside.

Then Big Yang stood on
the trolley, and climbed
out of the hollow tree.
He pulled the trolley
out after him.

"Thank you, Little Yin," said Big Yang, giving her a hug.
"Do you think you know the way home?"
"Oh yes," said Little Yin. She put the snugly and the
mittens in the trolley and slipped her hand into his.
"Shall we stop for berries on the way?" said Big Yang.
"Yes," said Little Yin. "Exploring makes you very hungry!"

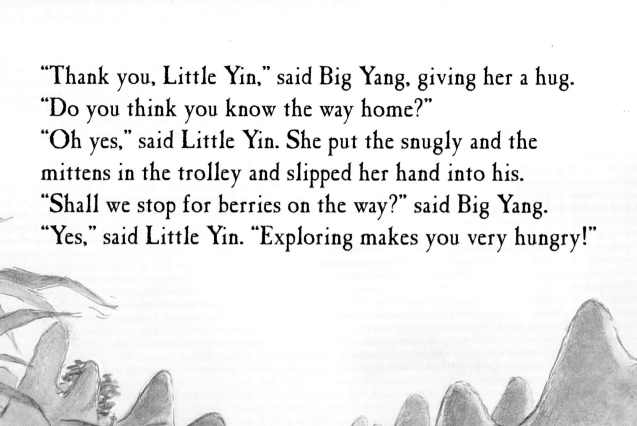

And with a yawn and a rumble of empty tummies
the two brave friends trundled home.